Gran's Gang

To King's Road
Primary
School

Best Wishes

Adam Tunnell

ADRIAN TOWNSEND

Gran's Gang

Illustrated by Kate Chesterton

First Published 2000 by
Grassy Hill Publishing
52 Wheatley Road, Garsington, Oxford, OX44 9ER

Reprinted 2002 twice, 2004, 2005

Text Copyright © 2000 Adrian Townsend
Illustrations Copyright © 2000 Kate Chesterton

ISBN 1-903569-00-1

Printed by Butler & Tanner Ltd, Frome and London

Contents

Gran's Gang

My Gran's got a gang. They all live

down our street and they're *trouble*.

My mum says she doesn't know

what to do. She's worried that Gran

will be 'put away' if she doesn't 'mend

her ways'.

Gran's good at mending things: socks,

jumpers and stuff like that. And she's

ever so good with wool.

She can knit anything you want but

I've never seen her 'mending her ways'.

Gran lives down the road at No. 52.

Next-door at 54 is Ethel. Across the road

at 61 is Winnie and next to her is Nora.

My Gran's name is Ada. *Ada, Nora,*

Winnie and *Ethel* that's Gran's gang.

Well, as I've said my Gran's good

at knitting but that's not all.

She performs in night clubs. She does

juggling, tells jokes and disco dances.

She stays out late. My mum says she

should 'retire gracefully' or 'get a proper

job'. Gran tells mum she's jealous and

that she should 'loosen up' or she'll

turn in to a prune. My mum hates

it when she's called a prune.

Once, mum got so angry she stormed

out of Gran's house and was nearly run

over by Ethel. Ethel was driving back

from the racetrack and didn't see mum.

You see, Ethel drives stock cars at the

local stadium and she's not a very

careful driver.

She builds the cars in her garage.

There's always lots of banging and

revving of engines. Sometimes there are

rude words as well when she hits her

fingers with a spanner.

Anyway, Ethel was returning from the *Demolition Derby* in her 'pride and joy' an old open top sports car and she just wasn't paying attention. Mum crossed her driveway and Ethel missed her by inches.

'Unethical Ethel', that's her racing name.

My mum says that Winnie is racy

but in a different way. Not just because

she races around a lot at basketball.

My mum says Winnie wears shorts

a lot just to flirt with the granddads

in our street. When she's not weaving

and dunking between the lampposts,

Winnie plays basketball in the local

Women's League. She plays centre

in the 'Silvergrey Goddess Giants'

(sponsored by Perma Wave hair

products).

Nora is Winnie's best mate and the

oldest member of the gang. She's also the fattest which makes it very dangerous when she's on her roller blades. She's still got a part-time job cleaning offices early in the mornings, when no one's around. That's when she roller blades to work.

My mum says Nora roller blades down the corridors of the offices she cleans.

"At least she's away from the kids there" says my mum.

"She's a menace on the pavement when the kids are about."

There you are then, Ada, Nora, Winnie and Ethel; Gran's gang. They're trouble.

Let me tell you some more about them.

The Police Call On Ethel

Last night was a bad night for Ethel.

Her best stock car *Bingo Bruiser* let her

down. Half way round the first bend

the engine gave up on her. Ethel was

furious. No more racing for the whole night. Ethel towed the car back to her garage. "No time like the present", Ethel said to herself. "Let's sort this flaming thing out." So Ethel went to work on the car. When she started it was about 9.30 at night. Gran was just going out to *The Silver Stars* nightclub to do some rapping and mixing.

Gran waved at Ethel as she passed by her garage. Ethel just muttered.

Ethel jacked up *Bingo Bruiser* and slid underneath.

"Just as I thought", said Ethel to herself.

"The differential has packed up.

I'll need a new one." So Ethel began

to take off the broken differential.

It wasn't easy and Ethel had to use her

No. 2 sprocket set and a big hammer.

Bang, bang, bang!

"Come on you devil let's be having you."

Even though she tried hard,

she couldn't budge it and she became

more and more angry. "You useless thing,

come on." Ethel cursed and swore and

banged and banged.

That was the beginning of the trouble.

It was getting late now and

Mr Wainwright, Ethel's next door

neighbour, was trying to get to sleep.

"Here she goes again", said

Mr Wainwright to his wife.

"That confounded woman is banging

and swearing when civilized people

should be asleep.

I'm going to have a word with her."

Mr Wainwright put on his dressing

gown and went downstairs. He shouted

over the garden fence to Ethel.

"Can't you do that some other time?

There are people trying to get to sleep.

Why don't you act your age and stop

annoying everyone. Now give it a rest

please."

Well, Ethel was in a bad mood anyway

but she hates being told to 'act her age'.

She doesn't much like Mr Wainwright

and she doesn't like being told what

to do.

"Oh go and water your potatoes",

she shouted at Mr Wainwright.

"Can't you see I've got more important

things to do than listen to you? Now go away and leave me alone".

Ethel carried on banging.

"You're a cantankerous inconsiderate old woman, Ethel", said Mr Wainwright. "If you were a man, I would come round there and show you *what for.*" Ethel threw down her spanner. She hates jibes about being a woman and old. She gets a lot of that at the racetrack.

"And if you weren't a miserable old nut case, I'd show you *what for,*" she said.

Mr Wainwright didn't like being called

miserable. He froze solid and looked Ethel straight in the eyes. "You…, you…, you…", and he walked away.

"That told him", said Ethel to herself and she went back to repairing *Bingo Bruiser*. Her argument with Mr Wainwright had given her new strength and with a bit more banging she removed the broken differential.

She looked at her watch. Half past midnight.

"The night's still young", thought Ethel. "I might as well adjust the track-rods while I'm about it", and she threw

open her tool box with a great clatter.

"The night hasn't been wasted after all.

This will be a good job done."

Now when Ethel is in a good mood,

she tends to play music … **loudly**.

She went to her sound system (with

surround speakers and a sub woofer).

There was only one thing for it; rap

music with a heavy bass. She found one

of Gran's rapping tapes (Club 74 studio

remix version), she put the tape on and

sang as she worked away.

She'd been banging and bopping

for about 15 minutes when she heard

a crash in the far corner of the garage.

Now Ethel is a strong woman not easily

scared, but she does have one

weakness; she still believes in ghosts

and late at night alone in the garage she

suddenly felt nervous. She stopped

adjusting the track-rods *'boom boom,*

gotta getta groove on down' went the

tape. Ethel listened. "It must have been

something falling over", Ethel said

to herself, "or that blessed cat from

 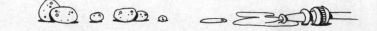

next door again. It's always poking its nose in places where it's not wanted."

She was just about to carry on her adjustments when **bang!** Something else moved in the garage. Then there was another crash and a tin of old screws fell off a shelf onto the floor. This was followed by another bang, this time on the top of the car. Ethel was underneath. She didn't like it.

She was scared.

Things were raining down on to the car; **Bang! Crash! Bump!** Ethel slid out from

underneath the car. She was now very frightened.

As she struggled to her feet, something whistled past her head. It hit the car radiator and stuck there. Ethel could see it was a potato.

Potatoes were flying in all directions. They were bouncing off the walls and rolling on the floor. Ethel took cover. Peeping from behind an oil drum she could see through the open garage doors. Mr Wainwright was on the other side of his garden fence.

 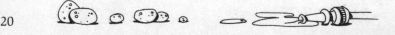

He had a sack of potatoes and he was
throwing them at her.

"Bombs away", he was shouting as he
threw. Ethel saw red.

"Right, that's it, you've gone too far you
old misery", she shouted
and she grabbed the nearest thing at
hand. It was the garden hose. She
turned the tap full on and aimed water
at Mr Wainwright. Then she put her
finger over the end of the hose to get
maximum pressure. "You're nothing but
a wet kipper. Get back into the sea!",

she shouted as she ran out of the garage

pulling the hose and aiming it at Mr

Wainwright. He ducked and jiggled

about in his garden trying to miss the

jet of water. Each time he did, he

grabbed a potato from his sack and

lobbed it at Ethel.

Maniac!

Misery!

Yob!

Potato head!

Ethel and Mr Wainwright shouted

insults as they dodged each other either

side of the garden fence. '*Boom, boom, gotta getta, gotta getta get on down*', went the stereo. Now Mrs Wainwright joined in from her upstairs bedroom window. "You're a shameless beatnik", she shouted at Ethel.

"Basil", (that's Mr Wainwright's name) "Basil let her have it. Give her what she deserves."

All the shouting and the din woke up the other neighbours. Lights went on in the upstairs windows of houses nearby as people looked out to see what was

happening. What they saw was an
incredible sight! Ethel dancing up and
down to the music, spraying water at
Mr Wainwright. Mr Wainwright in his
dressing gown, soaked to the skin,
throwing potatoes and Mrs Wainwright
leaning out of her bedroom window,
her hair in curlers, shaking her fists
and shouting. Well, eventually someone
called the police. Mr Wainwright and
Ethel were taken down to the police
station. Mr Wainwright was given
a warning and Ethel was 'bound over'

because the police 'knew her only too well'.

After a couple of days, Mr Wainwright and Ethel both laughed about what had happened.

Mr Wainwright said his vegetables were growing very well because they had never been so well watered before.

Ethel said she didn't have to shop for potatoes any more because Mr Wainwright had thrown at least six Sunday roasts at her. Mum laughed too when she first heard about it all. Then

she found out that the police had

confiscated Ethel's stereo with Gran's

rapping tape still inside it.

More incriminating evidence.

"Whatever next ?" said my mum.

Nora Races The Bus

Brr, brr, brr!

Five o'clock in the morning, Nora's

alarm clock was doing its best to wake

her. Nora doesn't really mind getting up

early, that's why she has her

job cleaning offices. The trouble is actually waking up. Nora is a very heavy sleeper. ***Brr, brr, brr!*** went the alarm clock again and then 'Good morning, another day of showers and sun shine'. Nora's second radio alarm had switched itself on and between the two of them they managed to wake her up. Nora rubbed her eyes and switched off the annoying buzzing. She left the radio on. She was waiting for the travel report. You see, Nora likes to make sure her way to work is clear. She hates traffic jams. She likes a clear run on her roller blades. If she has to dodge road works or other holdups it slows her down. Nora likes to go wherever she's going as quickly as she can. She is so keen not to slow down that she keeps lists of her times to work. The lists are plastered all over her kitchen walls. There's 'best time ever', and 'best time in the rain', 'best time carrying equipment' and 'best time (route modified)'.

She makes graphs of her

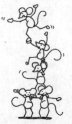

monthly roller blade times to work. For some reason March and April are the best months. Nora thinks it something to do with local wind conditions.

I like looking at Nora's graphs but my mum shrugs when she goes into Nora's kitchen. She says Nora is *obsessional*. Anyway, Nora likes to get to work as fast as she can on her blades. She starts her stopwatch as she pushes off from her gate and she stops it when she touches the front door of '*Malcolm and*

 *Malcolm Insurance Agents*',

the office she cleans. Fourteen minutes

27 seconds, that's her best ever time

and this morning Nora knows she has

to get very close to it. This morning is

special; it's the annual *Nora versus the*

Thene Valley Bus Company Race.

Nora and Harry Thistlewaite, the driver

of the 27B bus, race each other to Nora's

workplace. There is a five pound bet

to the winner and as well as the money,

there is the pride. You see, Nora has not

lost in the last four years and she wants

to make it five in a row.

Harry Thistlewaite lives around the corner from us and my mum says he's been driving buses for ever. Of course, she doesn't know about the annual bus and roller blade challenge. My mum thinks Harry fancies Nora because they go to Bingo together. I just think they are discussing the rules and tactics for the annual race.

The rules are quite simple. Anything goes as long as Harry stays in his bus and Nora stays on her roller blades.

 The race starts when Nora's

at her front gate and when Harry pulls

away from the bus stop across the street

just down from Nora's gate.

Now you would think that somebody

on roller blades wouldn't have a chance

racing a bus with an engine but Nora's

a brilliant roller blader. She knows all

the short cuts that the bus can't take.

And the bus has to stop at bus stops,

and go round a one-way system.

All these things make a big difference.

The last time Nora lost, she

blamed all the traffic lights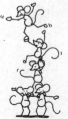

for staying green too long just as the

bus was approaching them.

She thought about writing to the

council or *paying* people to stand at the

bus stops to stop the bus but that would

have cost money and even Nora knew it

was a big cheat.

Five thirty and the news was on the

radio, nearly time.

Nora changed into her special 'Lycra'

shorts and top.

"I'm taking no chances today even if it

 is cold", she said to herself.

Nora picked up her roller blades. *Howson 29s*, they're brilliant, the best money can buy. She checked the clasps and gave each one a little polish with the tea towel in the kitchen. She couldn't resist blowing on the wheels. They spun round very easily. The special lubrication she put on last night was working a treat. No problems the equipment was fine.

Nora put on her knee and elbow pads walked out of her kitchen, locked the door and clamped on her blades. She fixed her helmet and glided to her front gate. She was ready.

So too was Harry Thistlewaite. He was collecting a fare one stop down the road. As he rounded the corner into our street he could see Mr and Mrs Wainwright waiting at the bus stop opposite Nora's house.

As soon as they were on the bus the

race could begin. Mrs Wainwright paid

for Mr Wainwright as they got on the

bus. As she did she dropped her bus-

pass. Harry got angry and told her to

move along. He had one eye on Nora

she was ready to push off as soon as

he moved into gear.

He didn't need Betty and Basil

Wainwright this morning especially

not Basil carrying a large garden gnome.

"It's got a bit of trouble. We need

to take it to the Gnome

Doctor", said Basil as they got on.

"We don't have to pay for him do we?"

He joked.

But Harry wasn't in the mood for jokes.

He told Basil to go and sit down and

hold tight.

Harry closed the door and shifted into

gear. They were off. Nora pushed

against her gate post and in a few

powerful strides was ahead of the bus.

She was going well along the pavement.

There was no one about, she'd got a

 clear run. If she could make

it to the corner in front of the bus she'd have had a good start. At the corner Nora was just in front. She turned left and Harry turned right, round the one-way street. Nora was pleased with her start but she wouldn't know how well she was doing until she could see the bus again in Norwood Avenue, after she had taken the first short cut through the shopping centre.

On she went through the deserted shopping arcade, past the fountain and down the new

wheel chair ramp and out of the
bottom entrance. That really helped.
The wheel chair ramp gave her more
speed and she pushed out into
Norwood Avenue. There was no sign of
the bus. Things were going well. She
pushed hard along the avenue dodging
the trees and keeping out of the cracks
on the pavement where workmen had
been laying cables. She didn't like the
cracks in the pavement so she jumped
onto the road. There was nothing about.
It was OK. She could go

faster on the road. She was near the top of the avenue when she heard the bus coming. Harry drove up right beside her grinning as he went. Nora could see his smiling face. He was holding up five fingers.

"Five of the best , £5", he shouted out of the window. Nora paid no attention. She kept her head down .

"He's not finished with me until the end of the avenue", Nora said to herself.

"He must have had a good start though."

She jumped back onto the pavement.

As she reached the top of Norwood

Avenue she cut the corner quickly.

Harry had to wait at the lights.

"Yes, yes that's got him." The lights had

just turned red.

Nora whizzed around the corner. Harry

had to stop suddenly. Nora could see

Betty Wainwright clutching her hat as

the bus came to a sudden stop.

"Steady on Harry", said Mr Wainwright.

"You nearly had my breakfast back

then. It's Norman Gnome

who's not well. You don't want to make

me sick as well do you?"

 'Silly old buffer', thought Harry.

The lights turned green, he was off

again. He could see Nora away in front

and he knew she would cross the road

in front of him into Willow Park Junior

School. Nora did just that. In through

the gate, opened specially for her by

George Carter the caretaker.

'I think he fancies her', thought Harry,

as he watched Nora zoom into

the school grounds. Nora

sped past the adventure playground, down a wheelchair ramp, across the netball court and out through the bottom gate into Kimble Road.

Nora knew that if she could get across the road and into the pathway that leads to All Saint's Church before she saw Harry turn the corner into Kimble Road she would make it.

Over the road she sped, into All Saints walk.

"Oh no! What are they doing here at  this hour of the morning and what are all those flowers?"

It was Mary Whitefleet from No. 69.

"And she's got a blooming cake", Nora
said to herself. "Oh no! Get out of the
way! Mind out vicar! Say your prayers
Mary I'm coming through." The vicar
peered over the top of his floral
decorations. Mary Whitefleet was close
behind. She heard Nora coming but she
couldn't see her. "Did you say something Vicar?" she asked. "Look out!"
was all she heard as Nora screamed
full-pelt towards them .

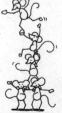

She managed to get past the vicar before she caught several flowers in the strap of her helmet. This made her spin and as she spun she clutched for something to hold on to. Only a cake came to hand. A beautiful two layer cake with white and blue icing with the words *'Life's a journey, not a race'* written on it. Nora's hand caught the top tier of the cake. Mary Whitefleet held on to the bottom part. The top tier flew through the air over the vicar's

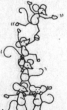 head and into his floral

arrangement. Chrysanthemums, carnations, roses and a squashed cake formed a new display. Red jam dripped down the vicar's hair.

'*Life's a race*' said, the icing. Nora couldn't stop. She knew that the vicar was still concentrating on his flowers. But Mary Whitefleet was spinning trying to hold on to the remains of the cake. They might not recognise who she was so she pushed off quickly down the pathway and out into Wellbourne Road. To the final stretch.

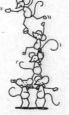

The last 100 metres to the finishing line.

Nora knew her collision had slowed her

down but she did not expect to see

Harry and the bus go past her as she

turned into Wellbourne Road.

Harry must have been doing 40 miles

per hour. Nora could see Mrs

Wainwright looking white and

frightened holding on tight in the bus.

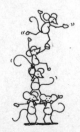

There were two other passengers

and they were holding onto the seats in

front and behind them.

Mr Wainwright had one hand on

Norman the Gnome and the

other on the back of his seat.

Nora could see he was red in the face
and shouting at Harry Thistlewaite.

Nora was beaten but she didn't give up.

She pushed on up Wellbourne Road.

She needed to cross it to get to the front

doors of *Malcolm and Malcolm*, the

finishing line.

The bus was in front of her now, at

least it was until Basil Wainwright stood

up inside it. "Slow down you maniac",

shouted Basil as he held onto Norman

Gnome.

 "This isn't Silverstone

Racetrack. You're a blooming menace this morning. My wife's going to have one of her turns if you don't ease up. What with that and old Norman Gnome here you've made his crack worse. If you don't ease up I'll … **watch out!**"

Harry had turned to look at Basil and taken his eyes off the road. He turned back to see Mrs Pymm crossing the road in front of him. She was on a Pelican crossing pushing her shopping basket with wheels on. She had pushed the Pelican light button but

not being able to see too well had

stepped straight out without waiting for

the lights to turn green.

Harry slammed on the brakes and Mrs

Wainwright's hat flew down the bus.

Basil ran to the front of the bus even

though he did not want to.

Norman the Gnome went with him but

he didn't stop when Basil did. Norman

the Gnome hit the windscreen, his head

broke off at the neck and rolled down

the steps near to the door. Harry and

 Basil looked at each other.

They were both red in the face. They looked at Norman's head on the floor and they looked out of the front window to see Nora gliding past Mrs Pymm on the Pelican crossing. She waved a full five fingered palm to both of them.

"Five fingers, £5", she shouted.

"I've won".

"What's she got to be happy about?"

shouted Basil Wainwright.

Later in the week, in the local paper, my

mum read about the bus company

introducing a complaints hotline.

"Oh I bet your Gran will be on to that"

she said.

Winnie Beats The Council

Winnie had sent off for some new

basketball trainers and they had just

arrived in the post. *Cool dudes 69* with

air cushions soles and pump up

support. They were seriously cool.

Winnie couldn't wait to use them.

She tried them on as she ate her

breakfast. They were light and very

comfortable. 'I'll have a practice as soon

as I've finished breakfast', Winnie

thought to herself. Being the centre in

the ladies basketball team is quite a

responsibility and Winnie takes it very

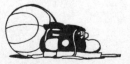

seriously. As well as practising every Thursday evening with the team, Winnie practises at home on her own every day. Outside, in her drive Winnie has got her own miniature basketball court. Her gate is the halfway line and down her drive she's got coloured lines marked out including the 'bucket' and back line right up to her garage. At the high point of her garage Winnie has her own basketball net and back board. She practices dribbling along the lines and spends hours taking shots into

the basket. That's why she's so good.

Her practice makes quite a bit of noise,

what with the 'pat, pat, pat' of the ball

on the drive and then the thump of the

ball on the back board. It's the sort

of thing that would usually annoy the

neighbours, but somehow none of them

seem to mind. Mr Goodyear says he

likes to see Winnie practicing.

Mr Woodward says it's wonderful that

she's still so active. Even Mr Wain-

wright agrees. He says he would rather

live next door to a fit basketball player

than a *Hot Rod greasy mechanic*. Mrs Wainwright doesn't agree. She doesn't like Winnie, especially dressed in shorts. 'Mutton dressed up as lamb' she says. Mr Wainwright says "Mutton can be very tasty." Winnie is popular with all the men in our street. Mr Goodyear painted the lines on her driveway with special paint and Mr Wainwright and Mr Woodward put Winnie's basketball net up for her. Even the young lads like Winnie. They call her 'Gorgeous Gran' and she lets some of them use her

basketball court sometimes.

Anyway, Winnie finished her breakfast, changed into her practice shorts and top and went out to her drive to practise. She bounced out in her new trainers.

"*Cooldude,* I'll be a cool dude when I score all those extra points thanks to these new trainers."

Winnie warmed up slowly. A few twists and turns. She saw Mr Wainwright smiling in his window. She smiled and waved at him. Mrs Wainwright frowned. After warm up Winnie

bounced and dribbled around the lines on the drive. "Yes!" The new trainers were great. Time for a few lay up shots.

Bounce,

bounce,

1, 2, 3.

"Basket !"

Winnie did 6 lay ups and got six baskets. Winnie and her new trainers were in top form. After lay ups Winnie liked to try penalty shots. She calmed herself, took aim and shot but **crack! bang! thump!** As her shot hit the

backboard her basketball net came crashing to the ground. The backboard split into two, worse still, the metal ring hit the ground first and cracked in half. "Oh fiddle sticks" said Winnie, "we've got a game on Thursday." Winnie was angry and was just wondering what to do when she saw Mr Wainwright running into her drive. He was huffing and puffing. "What a shame Winnie, what a shame, don't worry though I'll fix it for you."

He started to pick up the pieces when

another voice suggested it had fallen down because it was badly put up in the first place.

"I told you those screws weren't big enough Basil", said Mr Goodyear. "If you had let me do it Winnie you would have had a proper job not a botch it job like old Basil's here." "Who are you calling a bodger?" said Mr Wainwright. "You, you old fool."

"I'm not an old fool."

"You are."

"Boys, boys," Winnie interrupted,

"you're both very good to me. Please don't argue. I'm sure you'll be able to figure it out between you."

Mr Wainwright and Mr Goodyear calmed down as Winnie smiled at them.

"Well, I suppose I could make you a new back board", said Mr Goodyear.

"And I could weld you a new metal ring. In a couple of days it will be as good as new", said Mr Wainwright.

"Oh you're both wonderful, what would I do without you ?" said Winnie and she kissed them both on the cheek.

Mr Wainwright went pink.

"Thank you boys", she said. "You take the bits away with you. I'll get my tracksuit on and pop down to the sports centre and finish my practice there. I've got a game on Thursday. I might as well make use of my senior citizens' discount card at the sportscentre . The council doesn't do much for me but it can be useful today."

"Oh no it can't", said Mr Goodyear. "You can't use the sports centre today or the rest of the week. It's closed.

They're renovating the place, something about cracks in the roof and floor."

"What!" said Winnie unable to believe she would have nowhere to practise. "Useless, blooming useless, blooming Council, what do I pay my taxes for?"

Mr Goodyear and Mr Wainwright nodded. If there is one thing they all agree on it's how useless the council is.

"Right", said Winnie

"We'll see about this. I'm going to phone the council, we'll see, we'll see",

and she stormed indoors.

Mr Wainwright and Mr Goodyear had hardly finished picking up the wreckage of the basketball net when Winnie came storming back out of her house. "Answer phone, I got a blooming answer phone, can you believe it? It's supposed to be a help line. Press one for sewage, two for services. I'll give them a piece of my mind." and with that Winnie strode out of her drive still in her shorts with her basketball in her carrier bag.

"Oh Basil", Winnie called .

"Be a sweetie pull my back door up when you go. It's on the latch. I've got a key. Thanks sweetie."

Basil went pink again.

The council offices are at the side of the Town Hall right in the centre of town. Winnie arrived in a very bad mood. The bus journey had made her temper worse. The bus driver's joke about running a marathon and getting lost did not improve her temper. Winnie ran up the steps and into reception. The young

lady behind the desk was somewhat surprised to see a senior citizen in pink and powder blue basketball kit. "Can I help you?" she inquired.

"You certainly can", said Winnie and she bounced her basketball against the side of the counter.

"I want to see someone about the sports centre."

"I see", said the receptionist. "I'll see if Mr Charlton in recreational services can speak to you."

She picked up the telephone and after a

few words, directed Winnie along the corridor to office 16B. Winnie knocked on the door with her basketball.

"Come in", called Mr Charlton.

Mr Charlton was a small bald headed man and his jaw dropped when Winnie jumped into the office. "I want something done about the sports centre", began Winnie.

She went on and on and Mr Charlton could only take in a few words. 'Not good enough', 'pay taxes', 'poor services', 'in my day', 'too much money

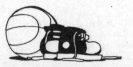

on foreign trips'. On and on Winnie
went. When she stopped Mr Charlton
was surprised and didn't know how
to respond. But at last he began with.
"Well thank you for your comments. We
at the Council take our duties seriously.
We like to provide best value to our
charge payers. We…"
and he began to talk some more, but
Winnie wasn't listening to him. She
looked at his little pink mouth moving
and his big bald head going pink.
He was ugly and he wasn't making any

sense. Winnie was about to shout at him when she looked past his pink ears out through the window behind him. She could see the main square in front of the Town Hall and she could see a large mass of tangled metal and coloured hoops in front of which were red, yellow and green lines painted on the pavement. A large sign said 'Art In The Community'. *'The man with the dream'*, a new modern sculpture by Daniel Freer, commissioned by your local council.

Winnie looked back at Mr Charlton and interrupted him.

"Thank you Mr Charlton, thank you very much. You have solved my problem. Thank you." Winnie hurried out of the building, down the steps, round the corner and into the square in front of the Town Hall. "Man with a dream", she was saying to herself.

 "He's perfect."

Winnie looked carefully at the statue. She couldn't work out what it was all about but she could see a shape

 like a man and she thought the man might be having a dream.

Whatever he was dreaming he was holding up a large ring with stars behind it.

"Perfect", said Winnie, "especially as it's got a backboard with it."

Winnie considered the backboard. She'd never seen one coloured blue

with yellow stars on before but it
would do.

Winnie took her ball out of her bag.
She hung the bag on the statue's
outstretched finger then began
practising dribbling around the coloured
lines in front of the statue. After a few
dribbles along the lines, she dribbled up
to the statue and shot her basketball
straight through the metal ring.

"Yes! One nil", said Winnie.

"This *man with the dream* is perfect."

Winnie continued to shoot her

basketball through the ring. Only a few of her shots bounced off the backboard.

"I'm shooting at the stars", joked Winnie.

After about 10 minutes, a sizable crowd had gathered in the square. People with shopping were standing still and workmen from across the road stopped work to watch Winnie. Every time Winnie scored, there was a loud applause and shouts of "Go for it Granny" and

"Yeah, yeah, yeah"

"Woo, woo, woo."

The noise spread into the council offices. It attracted the attention of George Webb the security guard. He came running down the steps in his blue uniform holding on to his cap. "You can't do that. Get away. That's a council work of art", he shouted. George was rather round and he could not run very fast but he hurried over to Winnie, pushing himself through the crowd.

"Oi! Stop that, stop that at once. You'll damage the stars. I'll have you arrested. Stop vandalising council property you, you under-dressed hooligan." George's last comment really annoyed Winnie. She was going to stop shooting into the ring but now George had upset her. She had made her point to the council about the closure of the sports centre, but she wasn't going to be shouted at like that from a fat, sweaty, little man in a ridiculous blue uniform.

"Come and get me lover boy", she

shouted back and she began to bounce

her ball all around the statue. George

wobbled after her shouting as he went

still clinging on to his cap. Winnie

ducked under the arms of '*The man*

with a dream'.

 George followed her but didn't quite

make it. His hat caught on '*The man*

with a dream's' finger and he fell flat on

his bottom. The crowd clapped and

cheered. Winnie took one last

triumphant shot at the ring.

"Goal! Straight in. No need for the

stars." Everyone cheered.

Just as George was getting to his feet he was relieved to see two policemen come round the corner into the square. Winnie recognised them. One was Frank Holder, the son of one of the members of her basketball team. "Come on Winnie", said Frank "enough of this. Now let's be having you."

My mum saw Winnie arrive home later in the police car still dressed in her basketball kit. She thought Winnie had had an accident and that the police

had given her a lift home.

 "Oh dear, it looks like Winnie's got hurt playing basketball.

Isn't it kind of the police to give her a lift home. Winnie is a strange one.

Still, it's a lot healthier playing basketball than your Gran's disco dancing. Poor Winnie", said mum.

Poor mum !

Ada's All-Night Rave

My Gran, if you remember is called Ada. It's an old fashioned name but Gran says,

"It's the only old fashioned thing about me." She hates to be thought of as old. That's why she goes to so many raves and late night dance clubs. She's very fit for her age and keeps up with all the latest fashions. She's got more of the latest fashions than me and my mum put together.

Anyway, Gran's always going clubbing and mum doesn't like it. She doesn't

like to think of Gran out late with lots of trendy young people. But last week Gran persuaded mum to go clubbing with her. It didn't work out well for mum but it did for Gran.

It all began when mum was round Gran's house helping her fill in a tax form or something. Gran was grumbling away about having to give her "hard earned money to the government" and mum was telling Gran not to be selfish, when somehow the subject of Billy Jay came up.

Billy Jay is an old craggy pop star with lots of hair. He smiles a lot and has loads of shiny teeth. He's been around since the dark ages. But he's my mum's favourite. She thinks he's wonderful. Whenever he's on TV she never misses him. She's got all his albums and loads of other stuff about him.

Well, the subject of Billy Jay came up as my mum was telling Gran off for going clubbing three nights a week.

"If you can't give it up why not cut it down to just one night a week", she

was saying. Gran was fed up with another lecture but she got back at mum wonderfully.

"Maybe you're right", she said with a twinkle in her eye.

"I'll cut it down to one night this week. Just Thursday, when Billy Jay makes his guest appearance at the *Silver Stars Club*."

"**Billy Jay**", said mum quickly. "What here at our local club?"

"Yes", said Gran "Thursday night, girlie's night special. Entrance by

special attraction ticket only and I've got a free pass. I bet you wish you had one prune?"

"Well for once you're right. I do wish I could go. If you're not too old, I'm certainly not and it would be wonderful to see Billy Jay close up."

"Well you're in luck prune. I've not only got one free pass, I've got five. The privileges of being a regular attender at the club. So you can come along if you want. The rest of the gang are coming. You can be the baby of the party, as

long as you don't cramp my style".

Mum didn't know what to say.

She desperately wanted to go but
she'd been clubbing with Gran once
before and didn't feel comfortable with
Ethel, Winnie and Nora all together.
They didn't always behave themselves.
Mum's love of Billy Jay got the better of
her and she agreed to go with Gran on
Thursday.

Wednesday was terrible. Mum was
washing and ironing all her wardrobe.
She got out every item of clothing she

had and tried them all on in different combinations.

"Oh that doesn't go", she kept saying. I had to tell her that bright jumpers are not the latest clubbing item. But eventually she settled on her own black dress and borrowed a top from Donna next door. I lent her some accessories and I have to say when Thursday night came she didn't look half bad, for a mum!

Gran had arranged for everyone to meet at her house. They were all going into

town in a taxi together.

You should have seen them all trying to get into the taxi without spoiling their outfits. Nora first tried getting in the door of the taxi backwards, that didn't work so she went round the other side. Winnie then got in first and took the seat that Nora was going to have. Ethel sat next to the driver and Winnie complained that *wasn't fair*. Then Gran forgot her clubbing bag and ran back indoors holding her hair so it didn't spoil. It was a real pantomime.

Eventually they all got in and it was in

the taxi that

Gran dropped her bombshell.

Not only was Billy Jay going to be at the

club, there was to be a TV crew there as

well. It would be filming Billy Jay and

the stylish disco dancer '**Ace-Ada**' my

Gran! Mum turned white. Not Gran on

the telly in her outrageous gear

cavorting around on the same bill as

Billy Jay.

When they got to the '*Silver Stars Club*'

Gran was helped out of the taxi by

Marcus the doorman.

"Hi yah Babe", he said to Gran and kissed her on the cheek.

"I hope you've got your red-hot bopping shoes on tonight". 'Oh good grief', thought mum, straightening her skirt before setting foot inside with Gran and her gang.

Inside it seemed darker than outside. At least it did until someone switched on flashing lights and a large laser beam shot across the ceiling. The music was so loud mum had to get right

up to Gran's ear and shout just to ask where the toilet was. Ethel suggested they should all start the evening with *'sidekicks splashes'*. This turned out to be a horrible tasting blue coloured drink with a straw and lots of fruit. As they walked through the club, people came up to Gran and waved and said, "Hi yah" and "Go Ada go."

Mum could see the TV crew. It focused its camera on Gran. Mum hid behind Winnie.

It wasn't long before Gran got into gear.

She took off her jacket and

went out on to the dance floor. She

pulled a young man out with her. He

didn't look too sure at first but soon

they were both dancing away as hard as

they could.

The camera followed Gran around the

dance floor and the DJ joined in.

"Come on you funky dancers join

the Ada alley." As he said this loads of

other people in the club came and

joined Gran and they made a line

holding each other's hips all around the

dance floor.
They were
followed
everywhere
by the camera
crew. Mum said
she just wished she could melt away.

This went on for what seemed like

hours. Mum had two dances with '*nice

young men*' and seven trips to the toilet.

When mum was seriously

thinking about going home the DJ

turned down the music and announced,

"The special event of the evening.

The appearance of

the legendary,

the greatest,

the icon,

the one and only,

Billy Jay."

Mum found herself cheering and

clapping like everyone else as Billy

Jay ran on to the dance floor. Everyone

was now watching Billy Jay. He was

handed a microphone and straight-away

burst into '*Only your eyes tonight*' one

of mum's favourite songs. Mum forgot about Gran and swooned as Billy Jay sang. Mum's wonderful feeling lasted three songs, in all about 15 minutes. It was after Billy Jay's third song that it all went wrong.

Billy Jay was singing on the dance floor which was made of shiny wood. It was circular like a race track. In the middle of the floor was a large round booth where the DJ sat. After each song he flicked switches inside his booth and lights and bubbles danced all around

the nightclub. People sitting near the

dance floor leaned over to try and pop

the bubbles. Mum looked around to see

if Nora, Ethel and Winnie were enjoying

the show but they were not there.

Suddenly, through the bubbles mum

could see Gran round the other side of

the dance floor. Just then the DJ

announced *"OK Clubbers, now we are*

in for a Thursday night treat.

Joining Billy Jay on stage tonight

our very own

gorgeous, mature,

club dancers,

Gran's Gang."

There was hooting, whistling and

clapping as mum watched Gran skip

out on to the dance floor dressed in a

pink miniskirt, blue top, tiara and

feather boa. She was followed by Ethel

in an orange boiler suit cut off at the

knees carrying a spanner and an oil

can. Winnie was next in her usual

basketball gear complete with ball.

Finally Nora appeared in a bikini top,

Lycra shorts and roller blades. The

people in the club went wild. Billy Jay
began singing 'As young as you are'.
Gran gyrated around him rubbing her
hair up and down his legs. Nora began
a circuit of the dance floor in her roller
blades. Winnie bounced the basketball
to the beat of the music and Ethel made
waving movements with her spanner
and oil can. The camera moved in close
up to Billy Jay, then Gran, then Ethel,
then Winnie and finally Nora
as she reappeared from the other side of
the DJ's booth on her second

circuit of the dance floor. The camera whizzed round to the happy faces of the crowd. It started to pan around to mum. She hid under the table.

Billy Jay was into his final chorus when mum looked out again. The DJ set off the flashing lights and the soap bubbles and that was a mistake. As the cloud of bubbles made its way towards Gran and Ethel, Winnie decided to try tricks with the basketball by bouncing it and popping bubbles at the same time. She lost concentration. The ball

struck the DJ's button controls and

more bubbles appeared .

People reached out to pop them. Nora

raced around the dance floor. As she did,

she tripped over an outstretched

bubble-popping arm. As she stumbled,

she looked for something to hold on to.

The *something* was Billy Jay.

She grabbed hold of his shirt. It ripped

open to reveal a white string vest. Billy

toppled backwards pushing

Ethel, who fell, squirting oil onto the

dance floor.

Even Gran's wonderful gyrating could not hold up on wet oil.

She fell, grabbing at Billy Jay's hair. His hair came away.

Billy Jay was completely bald.

He was as bald as an egg and he was wearing a string vest. As they all finally hit the floor Gran's miniskirt flew up her back, displaying her bright

orange knickers with a perfect white

triangular iron mark on the left cheek of

her bum.

The camera had it all.

Mum didn't say much to me at

breakfast on Friday morning. When I

asked her if she'd had a good time out

with Gran she just said, "All right."

When I got back from school in the

evening I noticed mum's

collection of Billy Jay records in a pile

in the garage.

Gran said she really enjoyed her hen

night out and that she was going to be in a TV documentary about disco dancing called 'Dancers Reveal Their Secrets.'

Actually Gran told me all the details of the evening.

I sometimes feel sorry for my mum. It must be hard being Gran's daughter because my Gran's special.

She's got a gang.

Gran's Gang

will be causing more trouble soon in their new book. You can read more about them at their very own website.

www.gransgang.com

If you enjoyed this book look out for other stories by the same author including:

Powerful Eyes

and

Naughty Lessons

Adrian Townsend

Lives in Oxford. He likes playing golf, football and dominoes as well as writing stories.
He supports Oxford United.

He can be contacted on E mail at

Hidip@aol.com

All of Adrian Townsend's books and other books published by Grassy Hill Books can be purchased on line at

www.Grassyhillbooks.com